Sunbeams from the Heart

A Collection of Twelve

Romantic Short Stories

Fay Knowles

"Hugely popular ... Charming and surprising": *The Lady* magazine, London, England, wrote about Fay Knowles' short story "Love at Sunset" which appears in **Sunbeams from the Heart**.

Love themes in this delightful collection of romantic short stories tell of nostalgia, bright new beginnings, homecoming, second chances, and unexpected love!

Connect with Fay Knowles at:
www.fayknowles.com

Acknowledgements

With gratitude to Tanya R. Taylor, author of both fiction and non-fiction books, who encouraged me to put this collection together. Most of her books have made Amazon's best-sellers' lists. Tanya helped me throughout the publishing process and designed the book's beautiful cover.

And with thanks to my husband Erskine and sons Gavin and Rory, for believing in me!

Cover Design:
Tanya R. Taylor
www.tanyaRtaylor.com

Contents

LOVE AT SUNSET

An elderly couple parked their cars behind sea lettuce hedges and strolled along the sun beaten esplanade arm in arm. A pink Bahamian sunset spread across the summer sky as the sea deepened to a shimmering indigo blue.

The pair sat on a bench under a gently swaying coconut tree, gazing thoughtfully across the sparkling sea until the sun had disappeared below the horizon. No words were necessary. They already knew what they were going to do.

"We must go now, darling," Violet told Gordon, "They might wonder where we are." Despite her advanced years, Violet's colonial genes had endowed her with very little grey hair, but Gordon had lost most of his.

"Nonsense, lassie," Gordon said. "We're not children." Despite several decades of living in the Bahamas, he still had a broad Scottish accent.

"Sandra says you're only after my money," Violet teased, "and that her Dad would turn over in his grave."

"My Ian says you'll never replace his mother," Gordon said, "but then he always was a 'Mummy's boy'."

Like a big bear, he wrapped his arms around Violet's small body. She responded with a cheeky kiss and he laughed with delight. Reluctantly they rose to their feet and headed back to their cars.

A few days later, Sandra dropped her children to Violet's luxury oceanfront condominium. She needed a babysitter while she and her husband played golf with friends.

"We're going to Paradise Island," Violet told her two grandchildren at the front door. She couldn't let them into her apartment. They'd find the place cleared out and her suitcases sitting inside the front door.

"I'll take you to see the fish," she said. Paradise Island with the Atlantis Resort's marine exhibits was just across the bridge.

The children could see fish any time they wanted. Their parents had a large yacht that took them from one end of the archipelago to the other. As far as they were concerned, a visit to marine life on Paradise Island was just for tourists.

They grumbled a bit, but Violet stood her ground.

That same day, Ian drove Gordon to a local sports club. A football match was being beamed from England on the satellite television. Gordon didn't let Ian into his flat either. That had been cleared out too, and suitcases sat in a corner of the living room.

"Thanks, Ian," he said when the younger man dropped him back home. "I know you'd rather not drag your old Dad along with you." Ian made a mild objection, but it was true. Ian was no family man, yet he occasionally felt obligated to spend some time with his aged father. At least, it kept the old man away from that witch.

On Monday, Violet met Gordon for lunch at a restaurant on the other side of town. They leaned towards each other, sipping iced tea.

"Here's your airline ticket." Violet handed Gordon an envelope.

Gordon winked at her. "Thanks lassie!"

"Is everything in place at your end?" she asked him.

"Yes," Gordon replied. "I'll leave my keys inside for the landlord. How about you?"

"I'll give my agent a set of keys. He's bringing someone to see the condo this afternoon."

"Make sure he's sworn to secrecy," Gordon reminded her. "My landlord is."

The next day the couple boarded a plane to Fort Lauderdale. They sat in separate seats, knowing how quickly news would spread to their families if they were seen going away together. They left their cars at the airport. Sandra and Ian could have them.

"Mum's visiting a friend in Lauderdale," Sandra told her husband. "She'd better behave herself."

On the third floor of an insurance company, Ian said to a colleague, "Dad's staying with a pal in Miami, so he's off my hands for a while."

"Is he taking that old girl with him?" the colleague enquired.

"You must be joking!" Ian retorted. "I told him to stay away from her or I'd put him in an old folk's home! That fixed him!"

After landing at Fort Lauderdale Airport, Violet and Gordon took a courtesy bus to the rental car terminal, and then drove to the beach.

They checked into a small oceanfront hotel, finally able to hold hands.

"Did you see that sweet old couple?" the front desk clerk asked her manager, as Violet and Gordon walked towards the elevator. "I hope I'm that happy with my husband when I get to their age!"

Once inside their room, Gordon embraced Violet. "At last, lassie!" They ordered a pizza for delivery to their room and each called home, to say they had arrived safely at their friends. "That'll keep them at bay for now," Violet said.

As night fell, they sat outside on their balcony, watching the moon illuminate the Florida sky and sea.

"Do you think we can do it, lass?" asked Gordon, grasping Violet's hand.

She smiled. Gordon looked into her eyes and imagined the beautiful young woman she had once been.

"My dear, they won't know until it's too late."

"And you'll do all this for me?" he asked lovingly.

"For us, dear. For us."

They made every minute count during the next few days, taking a cruise through the Everglades, visiting a butterfly farm, browsing the shops on Las Olas Boulevard – all things they could never before do together. And the most important thing they did was get married.

On Sunday, after breakfast in a nearby diner, Violet and Gordon checked out of their hotel.

An elderly couple walked down onto the long sandy beach. The man rolled up his trousers and the woman hoisted her skirt. They took their shoes off and strolled towards the breakers. A summer storm threatened. The sea churned with an undertow.

When Violet and Gordon didn't return to Nassau later that week, their families became concerned, but they couldn't reach the couple's friends.

"I'm going to the airport," Sandra told her husband, "to find out what happened." Ian was at the airline counter when she got there.

"Your parents took the same flight to Fort Lauderdale," the agent said. "But they were no shows on the return journey."

"It's your father's fault!" Sandra snapped at Ian. "If they're over there together, they probably had an accident."

"Don't blame my father," Ian responded. "Your mother's been putting ideas into Dad's head!"

Violet's friend finally answered the phone.

"She said they were in love," she told Sandra. "And that you didn't understand."

"I know where they were staying," Gordon's friend said when he returned Ian's call.

Shocked, Violet's daughter phoned the Fort Lauderdale hotel. "I'm sorry, they checked out on Sunday," the front desk clerk said.

Sandra and Ian flew to Fort Lauderdale and reported them missing. At one point, they stood together on the shore where Violet and Gordon had last been seen.

"We should have let them live their lives the way they wanted to," Ian sighed.

"It looks like they really loved each other," Sandra agreed tearfully.

Eventually, they returned to Nassau to await news from the Florida police.

The little Highland town bustled with tourists. A street bagpiper entertained passers-by, who dropped tips into a hat. It was a perfect summer's day.

An elderly couple sat on their porch at the loch side, drinking tea and eating Dundee cake. They would remain there until the sun went down, which was late in the evening at this time of the year.

"When do you think they'll find out what we've done?" the elderly man asked the elderly woman.

Her eyes sparkled. "Very soon, dear. Very soon."

** First published in the July 19th 2013 "Summer Collector's Edition" of *The Lady* magazine, London, England - www.lady.co.uk

THE CHRISTMAS SHELTER

That Christmas, when Tessa returned to the small town where her great aunt and uncle had spent most of their lives, the rooftops were white with snow. Shop windows glinted with decorations of reds and greens and golds and silvers. A Christmas tree with twinkling lights, shimmering garlands and a flashing star on top stood beside the town hall entrance. Outside, huddled together on the pavement, a small group of warmly wrapped people sung old familiar carols. But for Tessa it would be a bleak Christmas. Her dear Aunt Harriet had recently died, less than a year after her Uncle Leo passed away. Tessa felt as though the bottom had fallen out of her life.

Growing up, Tessa visited her elderly aunt and uncle whenever her widowed mother could afford the bus fare. Her mother had struggled since her father died and she was happy to send Tessa off to his relatives at every opportunity. Aunt Harriet and Uncle Leo were Tessa's shelter from the storm.

Her aunt and uncle had lived in a house called "Sunnyside". They never had any children, but they did have a tan Pekingese dog named "Max", who rarely left Aunt Harriet's side. They also owned a piano, which Tessa's aunt taught her to play.

Ivy covered the walls of Sunnyside and rhododendrons lined the driveway. Tessa loved Sunnyside's large rambling garden, with its apple orchard and the air raid shelter built in World War II. Uncle Leo had used the shelter for storage. And while he pottered around in his vegetable patch, Tessa would sit on the shelter's steps and read a book.

In winter, the holly trees with their bright red berries looked like a snapshot from a Christmas card. After a fall of snow, Max ploughed through the drifts with his short little legs, his long fluffy coat getting soggy, and his black nose and mouth a stark contrast to the dazzling white landscape.

When spring arrived, the wide kitchen window would suck in the sweet scent of blossoms from the garden. Aunt Harriet spent a lot of time in her kitchen, baking cakes, scones and pies that would challenge even a master chef. The local church fêtes were never without some of Harriet's goodies.

While Aunt Harriet churned the cake mixture with a wooden spoon, Tessa waited for her aunt to empty the large Willow patterned bowl, so she could scrape out what was left and lick the spoon.

They had breakfast in the kitchen, with Aunt Harriet heaping toast on the silver toast rack and serving homemade jam. Lunch at Sunnyside took place in the dining room, darkened by the monkey-puzzle tree, which peered through the window at them. Tea was on a trolley in the Indian-carpeted sitting room.

Tessa's uncle sometimes let her ride his old bicycle. She'd wobble along to the end of a narrow walled lane where a boy named Jimmy lived. He was the usual type of boy — hair unbrushed, grubby nails. Sometimes his rabbit escaped from behind the high stone wall and she'd help him find it.

"Hey, thanks," he'd say. "You want to see my hedgehog?" He'd pull the prickly creature out of his grey jumper.

She and Jimmy would often play in the shelter, pretending it was a fort or a pirate ship. When they became teenagers, they'd sit on the shelter's steps and chatter about everything young people chat about.

But Tessa grew up and enrolled in culinary school, so visits to her aunt and uncle became less frequent. Jimmy had gone away, to college, someone said. Tessa wished he was there, with his hedgehog and rabbit.

After Uncle Leo died peacefully in his sleep, Tessa attended the funeral, but she didn't see Jimmy.

The next time she stayed with Aunt Harriet, Max the Pekingese had become rather bad-tempered.

"He won't bite you, dear," her aunt laughed. "Take him for a walk."

Tessa led the crusty animal speedily, and at arm's length, up the lane and back.

That was her last holiday at Sunnyside. Aunt Harriet had a heart attack. A close relative inherited the house, the orchard, and the air raid shelter. However, the old lady left Tessa a generous sum of money. Tessa would now be able to help her mother. Harriet also willed the piano to her great niece. Again, Tessa didn't see Jimmy at the funeral.

On Tessa's return to the town, she found Aunt Harriet had made special provisions in her will for Max's care. "Your aunt thought so much of you, Tessa," the solicitor said, "that she left you the thing she cherished most - her dog Max." *Poor Max,* Tessa thought, *he must really be missing Aunt Harriet.*

"You can pick the dog up from the kennels down the road," the solicitor directed. "I'll have the piano shipped to you next week."

The kennels had exiled Max far beyond the other dogs.

"You came for that Pekingese, miss?" the manager asked Tessa. "Here's its kennel and lead. Can't say we'll miss him!"

The peke gave Tessa a little bark of recognition. His big round eyes begged her to take him and her heart melted. Max went quite happily into the kennel placed in her car.

Before leaving town, she drove towards Sunnyside. One more look, she thought.

She parked outside on the road and, leaving Max protesting loudly in the car, she crunched up the icy gravel driveway towards the monkey-puzzle, which bent under the weight of snow trapped on its branches. Red berries dotted the familiar holly trees.

The curtains downstairs were closed. Feeling like an intruder, she tiptoed to the back of the house. Peering through the kitchen window, everything seemed the same, except dear Aunt Harriet wasn't there with her mixing bowl.

Tessa walked across the lawn to the barren and neglected orchard. A mistletoe plant grew on one of the bare apple trees. She sat on the steps of the shelter, reminiscing.

She jumped as a voice came from above. "What's a nice girl doing in a place like this?"

It was "the boy", now a handsome young man, with sparkling blue eyes and well combed hair. "Jimmy!" she exclaimed.

"Sorry to startle you. I saw Max in the car and thought you were probably at the house." He offered her his hand and she stood up.

"It's really good to see you again," he said. "I'm sorry about your aunt and uncle."

"Thanks," she replied. She should have brushed her hair and put on some lipstick.

"I couldn't go to their funerals," he told her. "I was away both times."

"I do miss them."

"They were a nice old couple," he said.

They walked towards the front of the house, chatting as if the years had never come between them. Tessa said she was now a pastry chef. Jimmy had started his own pet shop.

As they approached Tessa's car, Max growled at Jimmy. She swung open the car door and the peke whimpered.

"He's become quite a miserable old mutt. I don't know what to do with him."

Jimmy smiled. "I think he needs a walk. Let's take him down the lane."

She opened the kennel door. Jimmy clipped the lead onto the dog's collar and lifted him wriggling onto the frosty ground. He crouched beside the quivering animal and stroked his ears. "Good boy, Max." The dog's tail wagged.

"You do have a way with animals."

"You have to get down to their level," he said, handing her the lead.

She knelt close to Jimmy and the dog.

"All he needs is love, like the rest of us." He winked at her.

Tessa stroked Max's ears and the tail wagged again.

Snow started to fall. Max sniffed at the flakes landing on his nose and shook his long hair to remove the white particles.

Jimmy took Tessa's hand and helped her up. The second time, she thought.

"You know," he teased, "I used to think of you as 'just the girl down the lane'!"

"And I thought of you as 'just the boy down the lane'!" Tessa laughed.

They set off on their walk, with Max pushing his way through the snowdrifts on the side of the lane. The snow fell more heavily, getting caught in Tessa's hair and feeling like cold little paws on her face.

"Just a minute," Jimmy said, taking her arm and stopping her from going any further. He gently brushed the snow from her hair with his hand. Smiling, he pulled something from his pocket. It was a piece of mistletoe. He held it over her head.

"I still believe in old traditions, don't you?" he asked. He drew her close and they kissed. Max barked sharply at them, jumping up and down in the snow with excitement.

Tessa had someone new to shelter her now, just in time for Christmas.

** First published in the December 12th 2014 special "Annual Edition" of *The Lady* magazine, London, England - www.lady.co.uk

CUPID KNOWS BEST

As the British Airways jet gained altitude, Kirsty peered down from her window seat at the patchwork of English countryside below. She should have been on her honeymoon. Stuart had booked flights to Nassau, Bahamas, for them. Then when he broke off their engagement and moved in with that glamorous P.A. from his law firm, he told Kirsty, condescendingly, "The trip is paid for. You can still go without me." Despite disbelief from family and friends, she accepted the offer. Now she was travelling on her own to a strange tropical island thousands of miles from home and she wasn't sure if she'd made the right decision.

A couple in the middle row cuddled and gazed lovingly into each other's eyes, oblivious to other passengers. *That could have been me and Stuart*, thought Kirsty. She had fallen for the tall, dark and handsome Stuart the first time she saw him, but his good looks had obscured her better judgement.

"Going on holiday?" a voice came from her left. She hadn't taken any notice of the man sitting next to her.

She glanced at him. He was about her age, athletic, with sun tipped hair and a tan, but rather nerdy glasses. Beneath the glasses he might be an okay guy, but she quickly put the thought out of her mind. She was in no hurry for another relationship.

"Just for a week," she replied, taking her magazine from the seat pocket.

"Nice magazine," he said, glancing at the cover of the equestrian publication. It depicted a woman horseback rider. "I like the picture. Who's the artist?"

"Me," she said hesitantly. "I work for the magazine."

His blue eyes, bright and honest behind the weird glasses, widened. "Really? I'm impressed." He told her he worked for an offshore bank in Nassau and had been visiting his parents near Oxford.

The seat belt sign pinged off. A communal sigh of relief rippled through the plane. A small child peeped over the seat in front of Kirsty, a mischievous look in his eyes. The man winked at the boy, who bobbed back down.

Kirsty couldn't help a little smile, but she closed her eyes and only opened them when a flight attendant pushed a food cart through the aisle. For the rest of the journey, she immersed herself in a book or slept, to avoid any further conversation.

The jet approached the island of New Providence in dazzling sunshine, descending over the turquoise sea towards majestic homes on white sandy beaches and glittering inland canals.

A long runway rushed up to meet them, heat rising from the asphalt.

"Good flight," her new acquaintance commented, as the plane powered down and moved into place at a gate. She nodded dismissively. Seat belts clicked and passengers pulled items from the overhead compartments.

Kirsty grabbed her carry-on from underneath the seat in front of her and stood up. She said a brief goodbye to her fellow passenger and joined the crush of people waiting for the exit doors to open.

She spotted him again in the terminal, when she retrieved her suitcase. He smiled at her. Then he was gone.

The hotel Stuart had originally booked for him and Kirsty stood tall and gleaming on what was sometimes referred to as the "Bahamian Riviera". After checking in, there was time for a swim before dusk, so she headed to the beach and dove into the crystal clear water.

Later she ordered room service and settled in for a long, lonely night. But when she awoke to a glorious tropical sunrise with palm trees swaying outside her window, she decided to make the best of her circumstances. After breakfast she caught a bus into town and browsed the luxury jewellery and fine china stores.

"Picking out your wedding set, miss?" a salesgirl surmised as Kirsty inspected an expensive arrangement of dinnerware. Of course, she was still wearing her engagement ring. She should have chucked it back at Stuart, but for some reason she hadn't.

"No," Kirsty said resolutely. She slipped the ring off and dropped it into her handbag.

In the days that followed, she took a tour of the island, snapped photos of marching pink flamingos, and sketched flowers, plants and trees at the local National Trust.

Two nights before she was due to return home she forced herself to go to the hotel's "Happy Hour". She soon relaxed with the cheerful tones of a Bahamian band and a large cocktail at the bar. Stuart was a million miles away.

"Enjoying yourself?" It was the guy from the plane, but he wasn't wearing glasses.

"How did you know I was staying here?"

"The label on your hand luggage," he said.

He hopped onto a stool next to her.

"Do you mind if I join you? I have to warn you though, I'm on the rebound."

Kirsty laughed. "Me too."

"Weren't you wearing an engagement ring on the plane?"

"Yes. When he broke it off with me I couldn't seem to let go."

"Well, I'm glad my curiosity got the better of me. By the way, I'm Paul."

"Kirsty," she smiled.

As the evening continued beyond the "Happy Hour", she found they had much more in common than she and Stuart ever had. She told him about her love of horses. She was never happier than when galloping across open fields or grooming her favourite animal. Paul had grown up riding. His mother had her own stables and riding school. He also painted landscapes in his spare time.

The band started to play a Merengue.

"Dance?" Paul asked.

Before Kirsty could reply, he took her hand and twirled her onto the dance floor.

Stuart had hated to dance.

After several fast numbers the band switched to an old Bahamian melody. Paul waltzed her outside and kissed her under a star filled sky. The sweet scent of jasmine drifted towards them.

Later he walked Kirsty to her room.

"I have an important meeting tomorrow," he said, giving her another kiss. "There's a lot going on at work, but I'll call you."

She spent the next morning buying souvenirs and the afternoon under a cabana on the hotel beach. There was no message from Paul when she got back.

She peeped into the hotel's "Happy Hour" that evening, but he wasn't there, so she went to her room. *They're all the same*, she thought angrily to herself.

The next day she used her last few hours to soak up the sun and that evening boarded her return flight to England, feeling let down again.

Someone lowered himself into the seat adjacent to her. "Whew, the plane nearly left without me!" It was Paul. "I was frantic I might miss you."

"What are you doing here?" Kirsty asked in annoyance.

"My firm is downsizing. I've been made redundant." He seemed cheerful. "I knew it might happen, so I was prepared."

"And you couldn't tell me that the other night?"

"Sorry, I wasn't sure and I didn't want to spoil such a perfect evening."

"You could have called."

"I left messages at your hotel yesterday and today. I also checked the Happy Hour last night, but you weren't there and I got no answer when I knocked on your door, so I went home to finish packing."

"I never received any messages," Kirsty said indignantly. "And after I didn't see you downstairs I spent the rest of the evening in my room." She relented a little.

"I suppose we somehow missed each other. Also, the hotel did tell me when I checked in that there were some technical problems with guests' voice mail."

"Well, I'm here now!" he teased. "And I managed to get a seat next to you."

The jet moved slowly away from the departure gate.

"Luckily, I have a new job offer," Paul told her. "My mother wants me to take charge of her riding school. My old employers gave me a good termination package that I'll use to invest in the business."

She listened intently.

"You mentioned you love horses. Are you happy in your job or can I persuade you to join me at the stables?" Kirsty hesitated.

"What about it?" he asked. "I need someone experienced with horses."

"That's an interesting proposition," said Kirsty. "Perhaps I could still do illustrations for the magazine part-time."

"Let's discuss it over dinner tomorrow," Paul said warmly.

"I think I'm free," she joked, plucking up courage to ask him what happened to the "nerdy" glasses he wore when she first met him.

He laughed. "I broke my glasses right before I headed to Heathrow for the Nassau flight. I didn't have time to get them repaired, so my father gave me an old pair of his."

Kirsty looked questioningly at him.

"I'm using contact lenses now," he explained. "I had a feeling appearance matters a lot to you."

"Not as much as you think," Kirsty smiled. She had thought she loved the handsome Stuart, but Cupid knew better.

** First published in the December 11th 2015 special "Annual Edition" of *The Lady* magazine, London, England – www.lady.co.uk

THE NEST

The rough edge of the packing crate dug into the child's legs. Sally kicked her heels against the wooden surface. Sunlight through bare windowpanes fell on the dusty floor and ran up the dated wallpaper. If only her mother were still alive. She would have turned the house into a real home.

She jumped down and plugged in the record player that had been one of the first things she'd unpacked. Then she placed the latest Elvis Presley hit on the turntable.

When the music started playing, Sally twirled around the room. She missed her ballet lessons. She picked up the last biscuit from the tea tray a neighbour had brought them. This was just one more kind gesture in their dreary existence of packing crates and fleeting acquaintances.

Men's voices bellowed from an upstairs bedroom. She'd continue the unpacking later. It hardly seemed worth it though. Her father would soon be restless again and they'd be moving on – to another town, another rented place. Sometimes she wished he wasn't so clever. He could always find a good job wherever they went.

"That belongs down here," she heard her father shout to the men.

She made her way outside to an enclosed back garden. A ladder that had seen better days leaned against high stone walls. A tall bush, with something nestled in its branches, grew in a corner of the overgrown lawn. She climbed the ladder until she reached the top of the wall and could look across at the bush. In it was a nest, with four little eggs.

A child's head popped up from the next-door neighbour's side of the wall.

"Hello, I'm Patricia." The girl clambered off a sturdy tree branch and sat close to Sally. "I saw you move in. What's your name?"

"Sally." She shushed Patricia and pointed at the bush. "There's a bird's nest over there. It has eggs in it."   "Ooh, yes," said Patricia. The two girls stared at the nest for a while.

"I only saw your dad move in with you," Patricia said. "Where's your mother?"

"She died," Sally answered.

"I'm sorry." Patricia sat quietly.

The girls dangled their legs over the wall. "How long ago?" asked Patricia.

"About two years. We used to have our own home, but my dad sold it."

Patricia changed the subject, digging dirt out of the wall with her fingernails. "I'm eleven," she said.   "Me too."

The children's heads turned at a flapping sound. The mother bird had descended onto the nest.

"Where are you, Sally?" Her father's voice echoed from inside the house.

"I'd better go," said Sally. She climbed down the ladder, taking care not to make any noise that might disturb the bird.

Her father was in the kitchen. "Come on, pumpkin," he said. "The movers have finished. Let's go and get some fish and chips."

She followed him into the living room. "I like it here, Dad."

"That's good." He ran his fingers around a photo of her mother that he had placed on the mantelpiece.

"There's a girl next door, same age as me. Her name's Patricia."

"That's nice."

"And there's a bush in the garden with a bird's nest and eggs."

Her father continued to gaze at the photo. "Do you remember the bird feeder your mum had?"

Sally missed her mother too, but Mum would not have expected him to grieve so long.

"I'm getting hungry, Dad," Sally reminded him.

"All right," her father said. "We'll leave the rest of the unpacking until tomorrow."

As they walked back from the fish and chip shop through streets that had started to empty of shoppers, Sally clutched the warm package of food, her father's arm around her shoulders. These were the special moments she enjoyed.

"Remember, when your mum was alive, we'd have some lovely walks on a summer's evening," he told her. The ghost had returned.

Before she went to sleep, Sally peered out of her bedroom window. In the moonlight, she could see the mother bird resting on the eggs. She felt very alone in the cold room.

She spread a blanket across the deep grass the next morning to lie down on and watch the mother bird on the nest. Patricia climbed over the wall and joined her. The children whispered to each other, keeping very still. Sally found out she would be going to the same school as Patricia. Her new friend took ballet lessons too.

Around mid-day, her father called Sally to come inside for lunch. She usually made the sandwiches, but they were never as good as her mother's had been.

"I'll see you tomorrow," Patricia told her, clambering back up the ladder.

"Sally, you should be helping me unpack," her father said, as they ate their lunch at the kitchen table. "The weekend will soon be over. You have school on Monday."

She nodded and poured some juice.

"It was easier when your mother was alive," he grumbled.

Patricia knocked at their front door the next day.

"Is that your friend?" her father asked.

"Yes," Sally said, peeping out of the window.

What's the point in me making new friends? she thought. She opened the front door. A pretty woman stood beside Patricia, holding a tray of tea and home made cakes.

"This is my mum," Patricia told her. "We brought you some more tea."

Sally's father gave the visitors a welcoming smile. Sally was pleased to see a spark of happiness in him.

"So that was you who brought the tea tray when we moved in?" he asked, rushing to take the tray from her.

"Yes," the woman said. "You were busy. I left it with one of the moving men."

"Well, thank you so much," her father said. "Come in. You both must join us." Sally was surprised at his good manners. He usually wasn't that sociable with anyone these days. Patricia's mother looked pleased.

The two adults chattered in the kitchen, putting out extra cups and plates, while the girls watched. "My dad seems to be getting on well with your mum," Sally whispered to Patricia. "Where's _your_ dad?"

"They're divorced. I don't see him much."

"Let's take our tea into the garden," Sally's father said. They followed him outside and he placed the tray on a wrought iron garden table.

"Hey, there's a bird's nest out here!" he said.

"I told you there was," Sally sighed.

A faint cheep came from the bush. The father bird fluttered nearby. Sally and Patricia giggled with excitement.

"Don't go near the nest," Sally's father warned them, "or the parent birds might abandon it."

He turned to Patricia's mother. 'I think I'll plant some flowers here and perhaps a vegetable garden as well.'

"There's no point," Sally interrupted, "unless we're staying."

Her father ignored the comment and carried on his conversation with Patricia's mother. "I must cut the lawn first though."

"I know you're very busy, with just moving in," the woman said to Sally's dad, "but could you come next door and give me some advice on my roses?"

Sally noticed that her father positively beamed. "I'll be more than happy to," he said. "And let me take the trays back for you."

The children stayed in the garden, watching the birds, until the grownups returned.

After that, Patricia's mother and Sally's father spent a lot of time together. Sometimes they would take the girls to the cinema. It was almost like when Sally's mother was alive, but of course no one could ever replace her mum. And her father made sure she knew that.

One day, Sally went to Patricia's ballet class with her, to see if she would like to join the dance school.

"I'm not sure, Dad," Sally told her father when Patricia's mother brought her home. "There's probably no point – unless we're staying."

"You know, Sally," her father gave Patricia's mother a big wink, "this house is for sale. I think we should stop moving and settle down." Patricia's mother smiled at him.

"And I'll have a real home again!" said Sally with excitement.

"Yes," her father laughed, "until one day you leave the nest!"

** First published in the June 20th 2014 edition of *The Lady* magazine, London, England - www.lady.co.uk

HOCUS-POCUS!

large group of tourists spilled out across Exeter's Cathedral Green in the early morning Spring sunshine. The majestic Cathedral towered on one side, with the elegant old Royal Clarence Hotel facing it on the other. New buds had popped out on the bare limbs of trees around the Green.

In good weather, Rachel liked to walk up Fore Street from her flat on the quay instead of taking her car, sidetracking through the Cathedral Yard before catching a bus to the hospital from the town centre.

Of course, some would say that nurses got enough exercise on the job, but Rachel loved to inhale the sights and sounds of the city on foot. It made her feel alive.

She had felt alive last month when Dr. Peter Murray, the most popular bachelor in the hospital, invited her out for dinner. Her hopes were dashed when after two more dates, he didn't ask her again. Then, on her way home from work on the bus, she had seen him seated in the window of a café, deep in conversation with a very exotic young woman. Rachel might have to accept that Pete preferred brunettes.

This morning she suddenly realized that with less than an hour before going on duty, she was practically out of cash. She walked rapidly through the narrow lane leading to the High Street. A cash machine was located near the bus stop.

"Want your fortune told, miss?" A large woman, wearing a bright green blouse, strands of necklaces and a thick brown cardigan with buttons missing, stood in her way. A wide red scarf wrapped around her ample waist secured the cardigan and held up a long, billowing skirt. Twisted braids dangled from a headscarf and patterned socks protruded from ill-fitting sandals.

"I'm in a hurry." Rachel tried to push past her, but the woman dodged back and forth, blocking her exit.

"It'll only take a minute, miss," the woman insisted, grabbing her hand. "Let Gypsy Lee tell your future!"

Rachel started to pull away, and then hesitated, remembering old superstitions. Her grandmother had warned her about gypsies, if in fact this woman really was a gypsy. "When I was young," Granny had said, "we couldn't refuse them if they came to our door. We had to buy something from them or they'd put a curse on us."

Rachel didn't want to take a chance. "All right," she relented to the woman, "but please be quick. I have to get to work."

The gypsy prodded the palm of Rachel's hand, and then grinned up at her. "I see a special man in your life." The woman drew deep breaths to emphasize her words, heavy bangles jangling around her wrists. Passers-by stared curiously at them. Rachel wished the alleyway would swallow her up.

Gypsy Lee peered closer at Rachel's palm. "He's a hard worker and a very caring man."

Rachel thought that description suited Pete well. Having seen him hold the tiny hand of a scared child in a hospital bed, or speak words of encouragement to an elderly patient, she knew how much he cared about his job.

"You think you've lost him," the woman went on. "But don't worry; he'll soon be back in your life again."

Only three dates, but it was enough for Rachel to think she and Pete might have a future together. All the kisses, flowers – and then nothing.

"Oh dear," the gypsy moaned. "Someone close to him died in a bad accident." Rachel immediately thought of Pete's mother. He had told her his mum was tragically killed in a car crash a few years before.

A crowd of people heading for the High Street stomped past them like a flash mob. Rachel noticed the buses at the other end of the lane had slowed down. She didn't want to get caught in a traffic jam and be late for work.

"Take him back!" the gypsy demanded. "He's the only one for you."

Rachel tried to pull her hand away from the woman's sticky fingers.

"Wait!" Gypsy Lee growled. "I see a wedding." The woman gave a dramatic sigh. "But it's not yours."

Rachel broke free. "I must go now!"

"That'll be five pounds!" the woman demanded.

"Five pounds!" Rachel was shocked, but she took her purse out of her bag. "I only have one pound on me."

The gypsy leaned back indignantly, hands on her wide hips. "I <u>know</u> you have more than that!"

Rachel clutched her bag defensively. "No I <u>don't</u>!" She dug in her purse for the pound and thrust the coin into the gypsy's outstretched hand! Then she fled down the lane towards the High Street, hoping the money would ward off any curses the woman might put on her!

She stopped at the cash machine, withdrew some money, and then ran to catch her bus. The gypsy's words ran through her head – "a special man …. very caring …. someone died …..". Just lucky guesses, of course.

The bus passed the road where she had lived when she first went into nursing. She had done well since then, moving from a bed-sit to the lovely little flat she now owned. This wasn't the first time a man had let her down, but who needed them? She had her moggy and she had her career.

The hospital buildings sparkled under clear blue skies today. As Rachel made her way towards the entrance, she smelled freshly cut grass and heard chirps in the trees. Hospital staff helped a young mother into a car with her new baby, the father brimming with pride. She thought for the millionth time how much she loved her job.

Later that day, on her lunch break, she was reading a book in one of the hospital snack bars when Pete appeared. He sat beside her, with an apologetic expression on his face and a bunch of daffodils in his hand. Her heart flipped and she put the book down. So much for getting on with her life without him, she thought. He handed her the daffodils.

She hesitated and then took them from him. "Thanks. How did you know these are my favourite?"

"I know more about you than you think!" He smiled and moved closer to her.

"I'm sorry I've been neglecting you," he said. "I had a bit of a shock the other day."

How could anyone stay mad at this man for long, with his sad brown eyes and tousled hair?

"My father might get married again," he said. He saw the look she gave him. "No, that's not why I was shocked – although it is in a way. A young woman called Lilly turned up at the hospital to see me."

Rachel shifted uncomfortably in her seat.

"She said she was searching for my Dad."

He explained that his father had an affair with Lilly's mother, Shan, when his dad did a short stint in Hong Kong. Pete was just a young boy.

"After Dad left, Shan found out she was pregnant for him," he told Rachel. "She gave birth to Lilly, but Dad didn't know, as he lost touch with Shan. And he never told my mum about the affair."

"So Lilly's the girl I saw you with?" she asked. He gave her a questioning glance.

"I spotted you in a café with her," Rachel explained. She smiled. "I thought you had a new girlfriend."

"Well, it turns out Lilly is my half sister! In fact, the only sister I have." He had mentioned to Rachel before that he was an only child.

"It was difficult coming to terms with it all," he said, "but I've forgiven my dad."

Some people sat down next to them and he lowered his voice. "Rachel, I know now how much I need you in my life, to help me through times like this."

Rachel held her breath. This was everything she had hoped for.

Pete said his father had gone to visit Lilly's mother in Hong Kong. "If it works out, he might ask Shan to marry him."

"Don't you think that's rather fast?" Rachel asked.

"Yes, I know it's quick," he said, "but Dad told me he and Mum weren't happy most of the time they were married. That was another whammy for me! I never knew."

Rachel gazed at him, misty eyed. These doctors worked so hard and had their own personal problems to deal with as well.

"Dad said Shan has been on his mind all these years." He hesitated. "I've given him my blessing."

"The best thing to do," Rachel agreed.

"I'd like you to meet Lilly."

"I'd love to meet her," Rachel said, with a little sniff. She could hardly contain her joy.

He smiled with relief and ignoring the people around them, kissed her. She dropped the daffodils in surprise. He picked them up and took her arm as they walked back to the wards together.

Rachel fumbled in her bag's zipped compartment for some tissues. When she pulled them out, a few coins fell onto the floor. She bent down to pick them up, suddenly remembering she'd hidden the pounds away for bus fares some time ago and completely forgotten about them - <u>four</u> pound coins, making a total of the <u>five</u> Gypsy Lee had insisted were in her bag!

** First published in the April 11th 2014 "Spring Collector's Edition" of *The Lady* magazine, London, England - www.lady.co.uk

BABY LOVE

New buds peeped out on tree branches and bobbing daffodils radiated sunshine along the footpath. Mothers strolled by with prams and pushchairs. Children's laughter in the playground competed with a chorus of birds overhead. "The kiss of the sun for pardon. The song of the birds for mirth," Jane thought, remembering the words of an old poem.

A man about her age joined her on the park bench where she had brought a picnic lunch in a wicker basket. It was mild enough to eat outdoors today instead of in her office cafeteria.

The man smiled at her. "I'm looking after my granddaughter," he said, pointing at a young child on a swing.

Jane nodded, retrieving a neatly wrapped sandwich and a flask of tea from her basket. She wished she had a grandchild to bring to the park, but the New Zealand air hadn't produced one for her yet and her daughter Nicole's time clock was running out. Jane was tired of people asking her if she had any grandchildren. Most of her friends were grandparents, which just rubbed salt into the wound.

Nicole had lived in New Zealand with her Kiwi husband Derek for many years. As always, Jane could hardly wait to see them next week when they arrived for their annual leave. Nicole was her only child.

The man pulled a loosely wrapped sandwich and a bottle of juice from a backpack. He wore an old hand knitted navy jumper, faded jeans and shabby shoes. He wasn't bad looking though. Kind brown eyes and grey streaked hair. She wondered who had made the clumsy sandwich for him.

The man's little granddaughter appeared at his side. She had a mass of curly hair and large dark eyes. Jane's heart melted.

"Papa, can we eat now?" the child asked.

The man placed his sandwich and juice on the bench and wiped the little girl's nose with a handkerchief. "Of course, Emma." The child clambered up and sat between him and Jane. Her grandfather pulled another badly wrapped sandwich and a juice bottle from the backpack.

"This is my granddaughter Emma," he told Jane, beaming with pride. "And I'm Paul." He looked questioningly at her with teasing eyes.

"Jane," she replied hesitantly.

"Emma has a cold, so my daughter

Sarah kept her home from school today." He unwrapped the sandwich and handed it to the child. "Sarah's a single mum, ever since her rotter of a husband left. I try to help all I can." This man appeared to be an open book, Jane thought. Not like her own rotter of a husband, who flew the coop a long time ago.

"I see you enjoy that," Jane said.

"Yes. When Sarah drops her by my place and goes to work, I give Emma her breakfast and make her lunch," he boasted. "I lost my wife three years ago, but I manage okay."

Jane glanced at his sandwiches. He saw the look. "Yes, I know. I'm not very domesticated, but Emma doesn't mind, do you, sweetheart?" Emma giggled.

"I'm taking you to see the boats afterwards, aren't I?" he asked the child. Little Emma giggled again. "I have a boatyard on the river," he told Jane. "She loves the sail boats."

Ah, Jane thought, that explained his rough appearance. She loved boats herself. Before getting married, she jumped at any opportunity to go sailing on the river estuary.

The three of them munched companionably on their sandwiches. Before she knew it, Jane had practically told Paul her whole life story, including that she didn't have any grandchildren and didn't think she ever would.

"Never mind," he consoled. "What's meant to be will be."

The next day it poured with rain and Jane lunched in the cafeteria. As she tried to listen to a colleague's chatter, her mind wandered to the park and the man in the hand knitted jumper. She wondered if she would see him and little Emma again.

It rained again the next day and the day after that, but by Saturday the weather improved. Jane took a walk through the park around lunchtime. There was no sign of Paul and Emma. The prams and pushchairs were out again, along with children's laughter.

She bought a posy of fresh flowers from the florist on her way home and placed them in a vase of water on the guest bedroom dresser. It was a bright spacious room. After her husband left she'd moved into the smaller bedroom.

She had spruced up the room for Nicole and Derek's arrival tomorrow and would take time off work to help make their stay enjoyable. Her daughter had a great sense of humour, but underneath there was always a sadness that she hadn't been able to have children.

Jane looked wistfully at the empty space along one of the walls, perfect for a baby's cot, and then shrugged off the thought. As Paul had said, "what's meant to be will be."

Later that afternoon she strolled along the river walk. It was almost high tide. Across the wide estuary a white sail bent in the wind. The small boat sped towards her and just as it seemed to be in danger of running up on the mud the sailor tacked. It was Paul. He held the tiller and mainsheet with one hand and waved at her with the other. "Meet me at my boat yard tomorrow afternoon," he shouted, "and I'll take you for a sail!"

"I can't!" she shouted back at him, shaking her head. "My family are arriving."

He laughed and waved again. Then he was gone.

The next morning, Jane waited on the railway platform for Nicole and Derek's train to arrive, the usual flutter of anticipation in her stomach. On the platform opposite, a teary-eyed woman held onto her parents, dreading the inevitable goodbye. In a few weeks' time Jane would be in the same position, saying farewell to Nicole and Derek as they headed back to New Zealand.

The locomotive, like a caterpillar, appeared in the distance. Her stomach churned even more. Within seconds the train arrived at the platform.

Jane looked anxiously up and down as the carriage doors opened and passengers spilled out. She spotted Derek dragging their luggage onto the platform and rushed up to him. He turned to help Nicole and it was then that Jane got the shock of her life. The couple lifted a pram out of the train. And in the pram was a small baby with ruddy cheeks and blue eyes that blinked at Jane!

"Surprise, Mum!" Nicole and Derek both said at the same time, hugging her.

"But how, when…?" Jane was aghast.

"This is your new grandson Ben," Nicole said with delight. The baby squirmed.

"How?" Jane repeated, bewildered but overjoyed.

Derek ushered them all away from the train, pulling their luggage behind him. "We adopted him in Auckland," he explained.

"And we wanted to surprise you,"

Nicole laughed.

Over dinner that evening, with baby Ben sleeping peacefully nearby, the new parents told Jane about the adoption process. It seemed to take forever, Nicole said, but all of a sudden they had the baby they'd always dreamed of.

"You really should have told me," Jane chided her daughter. "I'm happy for you though. He's beautiful."

"We have another surprise," Nicole said. "Derek has been offered a good job here. Ben and I will stay on with you after he goes back to ship everything over. Then he'll join us."

A few days later, while Nicole and Derek went house hunting, Jane took Ben for a walk in his pram. She carried a sandwich and flask of tea in her wicker basket. She wheeled the pram into the park and sat on the bench near the children's playground, smiling at the contented baby. Her life had changed in a flash. She now had her own precious grandchild and would have no more long separations from her family.

"Now what do we have here?" She turned to see Paul, along with Emma.

After Jane's breathless explanation and much excitement from Emma about the baby, Paul's granddaughter headed off to the swings. "Half term," Paul explained. He retrieved a loosely wrapped sandwich from his backpack. Jane took out her flask and neatly wrapped sandwich. Baby Ben gazed contentedly up at the new leaves appearing on the trees.

"About that sailing offer," Jane said.

Paul smiled. "As soon as you have a free moment from your little grandson."

* * First published in the March 27th 2015 "Essential Spring Collector's Edition" of *The Lady* magazine, London, England - www.lady.co.uk

THE FIRST MOVE

Charlotte loved her new job working in Aunt Annie's shop. She enjoyed arranging the tables and "Annie's Collectibles" sign outside on the wide sidewalk and chatting to passers-by as she displayed the goods for sale. Today though, Aunt Annie was attending a west coast antiques show and Charlotte was on her own.

It was a quiet community, with specialty stores dotted all along the boulevard where her aunt's business was located. Charlotte had recently returned to the small town where she'd been born and brought up to escape the fast city life. Her demanding position during the year she'd lived in New York had left her no time for a relationship. Now she was home again she hoped she might meet "Mr. Right".

"Hi Ms. Annie." It was the guy who called out to her every morning when he jogged by. He was really cute, with sandy hair and sparkling blue eyes. She wished he would pause a moment so she could explain she wasn't the Annie in "Annie's Collectibles". Aunt Annie was usually inside sorting out the shelves. If she'd had the opportunity, Charlotte might also have told the guy she loved to jog too, but all he did was flash that warm smile at her and speed on by.

"Why don't you think up an excuse to make him stop, so you can get to know him," her friend Brenda had said. "Perhaps ask him to help you lift one of the tables outside."

"No!" she told Brenda. "I believe the

man should always make the first move."
There was no way she would stop the jogger
in his tracks and start talking to him.

"That's why you're still single,"
Brenda who'd married her childhood
sweetheart said. "Look at that hot bank teller
I told you to strike up a conversation with.
You wouldn't do it and now he's been
transferred to another branch."

Aunt Annie had been more concerned
that Charlotte might not be able to manage
without her.

"Of course I can manage," Charlotte
assured her. It was an easy job, even though
the shop had lots of nooks and crannies and
rooms leading off other rooms that she had
to keep an eye on in addition to the tables on
the sidewalk. The one level building was
crammed with not only antiques, but also
second hand books, pictures, clothes, shoes,
jewellery, household goods and other
fascinating items.

Charlotte thought it was an easy job,

that is until later that morning when some tourists descended on the shop. She abandoned the tables on the sidewalk to follow the people inside. She retrieved earrings out of a glass cabinet for the women to see and showed the men some golf clubs, peeping over her shoulder all the time, to make sure no one had approached her displays outside. Of course, this wasn't the big city. She shouldn't need to worry about theft.

Charlotte smiled to herself. This was nothing like the pressures she'd experienced in her previous work place.

"Ms. Annie." She turned in surprise as the jogger appeared again. "I've just taken a cat down from one of your tables before he sent some glasses flying!"

Embarrassed, Charlotte rushed out to the front of the shop, with the jogger following. A black cat sat on the sidewalk purring.

"Oh, that's just Henry," she said. "He

belongs to an old lady down the road. He's really quite gentle."

The jogger looked at her with teasing eyes. "Well, it looks like you could use some help. I have a few minutes to spare before my shift at the gym."

Charlotte hated to admit she couldn't cope, especially to this good-looking guy.

"Oh, okay thanks," she relented. "I guess I could use some assistance."

"I'll watch the tables for you." He stood legs astride and arms folded, guarding Aunt Annie's goods while Charlotte served the tourists. After her customers left, she joined him outside.

"Thanks," she said, stroking Henry who was twisting himself around the jogger's ankles.

He held out his hand. "Tim."

"Charlotte," she said. He raised his eyebrows. "No, I'm not Annie," she laughed. "Annie is my aunt. She's away right now."

"Ah," he smiled. "That explains it. You seemed annoyed whenever I called out to you. That's why I never stopped before."

"Not annoyed," Charlotte said. "Just confused. I didn't have the chance to tell you I wasn't Annie."

"Well, now we've sorted that out would you like to get together some time?"

"What I'd really like," Charlotte said boldly, "if you don't mind another run today, is to go jogging. How about after I close up the shop?"

Perhaps she hadn't quite made the first move, but she had a feeling her newfound confidence might bring the romance she'd been hoping for. Brenda would be proud of her.

THE ROSE BOWER

A summer breeze ruffled Peggy's hair. She gazed upwards at the old Devon house, her home so many decades ago. It had been built sideways against a steep embankment and stood regally on its own above a row of terraced dwellings. Strangers would be living there now, but she had to see it one more time. After this trip down memory lane to the town of her birth, she'd need to find a new place to live. And soon. All of her worldly goods were on their way.

She climbed steps in front of the

walled property. Sadly, the radiant rose bower that once adorned the gate was no longer there.

"Can I help?" She turned as a handsome young man, with dark hair and brown eyes, approached from the house. Children's laughter came from a tent set up on the garden lawn.

"I hope you don't mind me looking," she said. "I used to live here."

He swung the gate open and gave her a broad smile. "When was that?"

Peggy squinted in the sun at him. "Over fifty years ago. This is my first visit to Devon since then."

He looked at her with interest and Peggy took an instant liking to him. So often all young people saw when they met her were grey hair and wrinkles.

"You must have been a baby when you left," he teased.

"I was seventeen when I emigrated to Australia with my parents," she said.

"I thought I detected an ozzie accent." She noticed garden soil on his shoes. Her father had spent a lot of time in the garden, planting flowers and vegetables, and of course tending to the rose bower, which was his pride and joy.

"I've just moved back from down under," she explained. "My husband died a few years ago." Tears still welled up when she spoke of Jim. "Then our daughter relocated to Aberdeen with her husband and children." Her only child and family being thousands of miles away had been difficult to bear.

"So you'll join them in Aberdeen?"

"I'm not sure," Peggy said. "I've always been quite independent. As long as I live an easy bus or train journey from them, that'll be okay."

He held out his hand. "My name's Tom. What's yours?" He had a firm grasp.

"Peggy."

"Come in and have a cup of tea,

Peggy," he said. "And you can see the house again."

As they walked past the tent, it swayed back and forwards with the movement of small bodies inside.

"Our boys," Tom grinned. "I'll let you meet them later."

The front door was open, allowing sunlight to flicker into the hallway. As they entered, she glanced at the staircase. The banisters might be the same ones she had slid down as a child when her parents weren't looking!

Tom led her through the house and into the conservatory on the other side. A pretty young woman looked up from pouring tea. An elderly man rose to his feet. He was slightly balding, an older version of Tom, with the same sparkling brown eyes.

Tom introduced them. "This is my wife Mary and my dad, Will." His father had a strong hand shake too.

"Peggy lived in this house before

emigrating to Australia in her teens," he told them. "She's just moved back."

"Do you think you and Tom's dad might have known each other?" Mary asked, glancing at Will.

Peggy looked at him. "I'm not sure. That was a long time ago, Will, wasn't it?" He nodded thoughtfully. She observed as she got older that often sagging jaws and sparse hair changed people's looks. This man had weathered time well though.

"I was born in a nursing home just down the road," Peggy told the family.

"That's retirement flats now," Will said. "I live in one of them." He pulled out a chair for Peggy to sit down. "How long are you here for?"

"Just another night," she said. "I flew in yesterday and I came right down here. I wanted to see the town again before heading north to my daughter and family."

"Do you remember the old haunts?" Will asked. "The Odeon, the coffee bars...?"

"Have some tea first," Mary interrupted, "before you two start reminiscing." She poured a cup for Peggy and passed her the milk and sugar.

"Dad gets lonely since losing Tom's mum a couple of years ago, so we often have him over," she told her in a low voice.

"I understand," Peggy said. "I'm a widow."

She turned to Will. "Yes, I do remember the coffee bars and The Odeon." A boy once took her to see the romantic film *A Summer Place* at The Odeon and bought her a Cadbury's "Sliced Nut", a favourite at the time. It was a custom then for a girl's date to buy her a chocolate bar before the film started and walk her home afterwards.

"There used to be a field next to the house, level with the bedrooms," Peggy said.

"Nothing's changed," said Tom. "No one ever built on it."

Peggy smiled. "I'm glad. The sheep

used to gather at my bedroom window."

"And they still do," Mary laughed. "It's our sons' bedroom now."

"Would you like to see it again?" asked Tom.

They climbed the stairs and Peggy followed the family into the children's bedroom. The boys obviously had a tussle with their pillows.

"Sorry about the mess," Mary said, picking the pillows up from the floor. "You know how boys are!"

The children's two tiered bunk beds with football design duvets lined the same wall where Peggy's frilly pink bed had been. She peered out of the window. Sheep munched their way across the field.

She often dreamed about her old bedroom and now here she was. She could hardly contain her excitement.

"Dad, why not take Peggy for a walk down to the stream?" Tom suggested.

"I would love that," Peggy said.

Will beckoned to her and she climbed through the window and onto the field, with little effort. Those years of swimming and tennis had paid off. Will followed just as nimbly.

"So you came here before going to your family?" Will commented.

"Unfortunately, my timing was a bit off," Peggy replied. "They're in Spain on holiday and not returning until tomorrow."

They manoeuvred their way between the sheep and across the grass. "Anyway," Peggy said, "I'm glad I had a chance to come down here first."

They clambered over a stile and walked through long grass to a slope leading down to the stream.

"I remember primroses blooming all over this bank," Peggy said. "My friends and I used to pick bunches of them to take home."

"Yes, they're abundant here in season," Will agreed. "We had a lovely show of them this year."

They sat on a log, gazing down through the gulley. The water trickled in some places, and then built up to a crescendo as large boulders blocked it, crashing downwards when it escaped.

"Such a beautiful spot," Peggy sighed. "So many memories."

Will helped her to her feet and they made their way back to the house.

"Hurry," he joked. "There's an old ram looking at us rather strangely over there!"

They arrived back at the house, laughing about the perils and pleasures of country life.

Over another cup of tea, Peggy said her daughter wanted her to settle in Aberdeen near her. "I haven't decided yet though. I'd like to buy a little flat somewhere quiet and peaceful."

With sunlight fading in the conservatory, Peggy said she must leave. "I'm staying in a bed and breakfast on the quay. Then I have a bus to catch in the morning."

They walked her to the gate and the children emerged from the tent. "This lady lived here when she was a little girl," Mary told her sons.

The boys' beaming faces looked up at Peggy as they hung onto their mum. Peggy realized how much she was looking forward to seeing her grandchildren again.

"Have you considered coming back here to live?" Will asked. "It has what you're looking for – peace and quiet!"

"That's a possibility," Peggy said. He smiled.

"We can put you in touch with a good estate agent," Mary offered.

"I used to be a building inspector," Will said. "I'd be happy to check the properties out for you. In fact, let me walk you down to the quay and we can talk more about it."

Things were starting to look better by

the minute, Peggy thought. Will had a certain charm and mischievous sense of humour. She could just picture meeting him and a bunch of seniors in the town for a regular morning coffee. And her daughter could bring the children down on their school breaks. It would be a nice life.

"I'll see what my daughter thinks," said Peggy. "She might enjoy holidays in Devon!"

Will leaned on the gate, with a thoughtful expression again. "Tom, a long time ago, before you and Mary bought this house, there was a beautiful rose bower here. You should erect another one," he said to his son.

"You remember the rose bower?" Peggy asked in surprise.

"Yes," Will said, winking at her. "And I remember you! You kissed me goodbye under the rose bower when I walked you home from The Odeon. After we saw that great film *A Summer Place*!"

* * First published in the July 18th 2014 "Summer Collector's Edition" of *The Lady* magazine, London, England - www.lady.co.uk

CLOSET MAGIC

"**A**re you ready, Chloe?" Michelle strutted up and down the hallway, her high heels tapping. "We have a new client. He wants to give the special woman in his life one of our closet makeovers. It's her birthday."

"I'll be there in a minute." Chloe whisked the sawdust off the floor and put the hammer in her tool belt.

"Hurry," Michelle called. Chloe's old school friend Michelle was a hard taskmaster when it came down to their business as closet consultants.

"I'll drive." As usual, Michelle was in control. Chloe dragged her ladder and equipment to the van and threw them into the back. "I'm finished," she told Michelle. "It's up to you now."

Michelle locked the front door. "Don't worry about that," she laughed. "Would I ever let you down?"

Chloe knew she wouldn't. Michelle was a fashion diva and could plan an entire new wardrobe of clothes for clients. Chloe's job was to rip out shelves and remodel the closets.

Jeff Harper was waiting for them outside a detached house at the end of a cul-de-sac. "She had to leave," he explained, smiling at both women, "but you should go ahead anyway."

Chloe wiped her hands on her jeans, wishing she'd had time to freshen up, but this was pretty much the way her life had always been. She'd grown up as a tomboy and that's how men still seemed to regard her.

She fingered her ponytail as Michelle introduced them: "This is my business partner Chloe." Of course, glamorous Michelle captivated all the guys who came into their lives. And this guy was the best looking one she'd seen in a while. As usual, it seemed he was spoken for.

"Did Michelle explain all the plans we offer?" Chloe asked him, tucking strands of brown hair behind her ears. "Yes, I did," Michelle intervened.

"I want the best," Jeff emphasized. He was quite classy himself, sleeves rolled up and shirt open at the neck, as if he'd just come from a gruelling board meeting.

"Show us the way," Chloe told him.

The walk-in closet of this special woman in his life had doors hanging on their hinges and rails laden with clothes. Mismatched shoes tumbled onto the floor from scratched and uneven shelves.

"First of all," Michelle said, "everything has to come out of the closet. I'll take it away and sift through it, to see what can be rescued." She looked directly into Jeff's eyes. "She does realize that she may never see some of these things again?" Jeff nodded.

"While Michelle is dealing with that," Chloe told him, "I'll do a major overhaul of the closet."

"I'll stop by later then." Jeff winked. "I have to get back to my office, but I know I can count on you girls."

Michelle piled everything from the closet into the van and sped off. Chloe got to work, using all the skills she had learned in her apprenticeship to a master carpenter.

A few hours later, she had finished the renovations. She glimpsed her reflection in the closet mirror. What a mess she looked. She pulled a brush from her bag and released the ponytail. Her hair spilled onto her shoulders. Then she retrieved some rarely used make up from her handbag and went into the bathroom to apply it.

The front door slammed. "Wow!" Jeff exclaimed, walking into the refitted closet. "It looks great."

"Glad you like it, Mr. Harper." He turned in surprise as Chloe appeared, her hair flowing and eyes sparkling. "I still have some cleaning up to do," she told him.

"It's five o'clock," he argued. "Time to stop work. And call me Jeff."

"But everything must be perfect when your girlfriend gets home," she protested.

"It *is* perfect," he smiled. "And it's not my girlfriend's closet. It's my mum's!"

"Your mum?" Chloe asked in surprise.

"Yes, of course," Jeff said. "Who did you think you were redesigning the closet for?"

"Michelle said it was for the special woman in your life," Chloe stammered.

"That's absolutely right," Jeff laughed. "My mum is the only woman in my life right now. But that could change if you let me take you to dinner tonight."

THE PERFECT MATCH

"Come on, Gran," Celeste beckoned to Doreen. "Let's get to work!" Celeste had positioned herself in front of her grandmother's computer. Doreen would much rather relax outside in her garden chair with a book, inhale the sweet scent of summer blooms and watch her little feathered friends dip into the stone birdbath. Sometimes she just sat and reminisced about all the happy years she and Harry had spent together before a heart attack ripped him away from her.

Celeste had stopped by that Saturday to give her grandmother a lesson on how to use the computer, which was a gift from Doreen's son. Doreen loved to see the young woman, but wished Celeste had a boyfriend to spend weekends with. Of course, if Celeste had a man in her life, he'd have to share her with modern technology. The girl was addicted to her work.

"Come and boot up, Gran," Celeste called to her.

Doreen joined Celeste and switched on the computer. She didn't have any problem with basic functions. She used to be a secretary. It was the rest of it that was more difficult.

"Don't you get lonely sometimes, Gran?" Celeste asked.

"Not really," Doreen said. Of course, it was difficult at first when Harry died, but she had moved near her son and family and gradually slipped into a pleasant routine of strolling down to the village with her shopping basket in the mornings and taking a bus into the city after lunch, to browse Marks and Spencer or C&A. Then in the evenings she'd watch her favourite programmes on the television, the same ones she and Harry used to watch together.

"Wouldn't it be good to meet a man around your age, to go on outings or have dinner with?" Celeste asked.

"It's you who should be looking for a man, Celeste."

"Gran, I don't have time. Anyway, all the men I know are only interested in football or the pub."

Doreen sighed. Perhaps her granddaughter's brains got in the way of her beauty.

Celeste brought up a website on the computer. "You could meet someone through this dating site," she said. "I know someone who found a really decent guy on it."

"Your grandfather would turn over in his grave!"

"I'm sure Granddad would want you to be happy," Celeste said. "And it's been a long time now since he passed away."

Doreen started to argue again, but then had an idea. Perhaps if she joined the dating site Celeste might too.

Celeste's fingers moved over the keyboard so fast they were just a blur. "I'm going to create an account for you. It's quite easy."

"What will I do if a man contacts me?" Doreen asked.

"Don't worry, Gran, I'll help you."

Doreen peered at the screen, as Celeste typed in a user name for her grandmother and added a photo of Doreen that she found on the computer.

"Now all I have to do is complete a questionnaire for you and we'll be done."

Celeste stopped by again after work a few days later, but refused to join the dating site herself. "Don't worry, Gran, the right guy for me will turn up at the right time."

Doreen wasn't so sure about that. If Celeste didn't stop being such a workaholic she might miss the "right guy". She pressed the computer's power button and pulled up a chair for her granddaughter.

"Look Gran. You already have two replies."

Doreen peered at the photos that came up on the screen.

"This one is younger than you, Gran! He must think you're a cougar!"

"A cougar?"

"Older women who prey on younger men!"

Doreen was horrified.

"That's okay, Gran," Celeste laughed. "We'll delete him. This other one looks hopeful though. He's a widower."

By Friday, Doreen had messaged back and forwards twice with a Mr. Tony Brown. He was about her age and liked gardening.

"He sounds perfect," said Celeste, when she popped in that evening.

"He wants to meet me, Celeste."

"That's great!" Her granddaughter was ecstatic. "Say yes!"

Doreen hesitated, but continued with the charade. And she had to admit, this dating game did bring some excitement into her life.

"Don't worry, I'll come along with you to check him out," Celeste said.

"Okay, I'll meet him, but only if you agree to join the dating site too."

"Okay, Gran. Later," Celeste relented.

That Saturday morning, Doreen and Celeste sat in a café, drinking coffee and waiting for Mr. Tony Brown to arrive. To her grandmother's disappointment, Celeste still hadn't signed up on the matchmaking website.

Doreen looked at her watch. "He's late."

"Give him a little more time, Gran." Celeste took out her phone. "I might as well check my emails while we're waiting."

Celeste tapped on the phone for a few seconds. "Darn," she exclaimed, "I can't get online."

A thin young man at a nearby table turned towards them. "The internet's down, but the manager said it will be up again soon."

He was about Celeste's age, Doreen thought, with quirky glasses, frayed jeans and a laptop. He didn't fit the mould she had in mind for her granddaughter, of a smart young man with perfect biceps and a large bank account.

"Quirky" and Celeste soon struck up a conversation about computer technology, way above Doreen's head. Another geek, Doreen thought.

"Okay, we're online again," he said. Smiling at Celeste he turned back to his laptop.

"Well, Celeste," said Doreen, "I really think we should leave. Mr. Brown is far too late." Before Celeste could answer, an elderly man hurried in. Doreen recognized him from his photo on the dating site, but he just rushed past them, looking worried.

He joined Quirky at the table next to them. "Sorry I'm late, Mike. Road works." Then recognition set in as he looked towards Doreen.

"That's okay, Granddad, I think the lady you're meeting is still here." The grandson winked at Doreen and stood up. He took his grandfather's arm and steered him towards her. "Are you waiting for a Mr. Tony Brown?"

Doreen nodded. Celeste quickly intervened. "Yes, she is!"

"This is Tony Brown. I'm Mike."

The older man smiled at Doreen.

"I helped Granddad hook up online with this lovely lady," Mike told Celeste.

"And I helped my grandmother connect with your granddad!" Celeste bubbled over.

They all decided to have lunch together. Celeste and Mike prattled on to each other about cyber space and Tony told Doreen he belonged to the National Trust. "Perhaps you'd like to see one of the gardens with me?" he suggested to Doreen.

Celeste's eyes twinkled. Mike's eyes twinkled too and he turned to Celeste. "How about having dinner with me tonight?"

Doreen smiled with satisfaction. Perhaps Mike did fit the mould after all. And Mr. Tony Brown didn't seem too bad either!

** Also published in the March 18th – 31st 2016

"Spring Collector's Edition" of *The Lady* magazine,

London, England – www.lady.co.uk

ENGLISH ROSE

He shuffled to the table and picked up a well-chewed pen. Grasping the pen in one large hand and a yellow lined pad with torn edges in the other, he eased himself into a chair to start work on his novel. Outside it was a typically English rainy day.

The book would be a romance. Of course, he'd throw in some suspense as well. He scribbled a few words, and then pushed himself to his feet, muttering. A real author couldn't write without inspiration. He made his way to the window.

He observed a slim young woman in a shiny blue raincoat scurrying along a path on the other side of the deep embankment. Blond hair spilled from her hood. Skidding on damp fallen leaves, she quickly caught her balance.

Within minutes, she melted into a backdrop of orange and gold. He strained his eyes to look for her, but she had gone. A Marilyn Monroe, a Grace Kelly …. a Princess Diana. She had brought sunshine into his confined existence.

A few days later, he glimpsed her again. She stamped through a torrential downpour of rain, water splattering from her boots. She unfurled an umbrella defiantly in front of her as the wind swirled and changed direction. Then she darted out of sight.

She seemed in a hurry to get

somewhere, but he knew it was fate that took her along that isolated path.

He picked up his pad and pen. The novel was going well.

Another week passed. The weather had improved and he heard the sound of a combine in a nearby field. He started to sneeze and swallowed a pill.

The next time she rushed past, he almost called out, but his voice wouldn't have carried that far. He shook his head and grabbed his pen in frustration.

It was now late autumn, with its warning of bleak winter days. He cheered up when he spotted the young woman again. She'd stuffed her hair into a bright red beret. A long skirt billowed around her ankles. He grabbed another yellow pad and his pen took over.

Winter was here. He looked for her beneath the naked branches of the trees across the embankment. Then she reappeared, wearing a snug black coat, her blond hair loose.

Christmas was desolate for him. She was nowhere to be seen. 'Silent night - ', he heard the faint strains of a Salvation Army band in the distance.

The weeks went by. He felt he was going crazy, not seeing her. Writing his book was the only thing that kept him sane. Then new buds burst out on the trees and birds sang. He called the novel "English Rose".

And there she was at long last, his "English Rose", dressed in a pretty floral dress. She paused and looked up at him. Yes, he was sure she was staring at him, but she seemed annoyed.

On the other side of the ravine, Caroline tripped along the path below the beech trees. She smiled to herself for she would soon be married to the greatest guy in the world.

Glancing up at a distant window above the embankment, she hesitated. She thought she saw a man's face, peering at her. She shuddered. She wouldn't take this short cut to work anymore. In future, she would always leave home on time.

He watched her until she was out of sight. Days went by and then weeks. Finally, as summer drew to a close he accepted that she would never be coming back. With a deep sigh, he scribbled the last few lines of his novel and wrote the words "The End".

* * First published in the July/August 2015 issue of *The Broadkill Review*, Delaware, U.S.A. - www.thebroadkillriverpress.com/the-broadkill-review

CHRISTMAS IN PARADISE
Sequel to short story
"Love at Sunset"

An elderly woman with a wide brimmed millinery creation that masked her eyes dropped some dollar notes into a Salvation Army Christmas kettle and entered a luxury jewellery store on Nassau's old downtown Bay Street. She was followed by a dapper elderly man in a Panama hat, his nose and cheeks ruddy from sudden exposure to the tropical sun.

Bell ringers stood at strategic points, collecting money for charity in the kettles. Bay Street was decked out with festive decorations. A heavily laden Christmas tree towered next to the Colonial buildings in historic Rawson Square and bleachers for the upcoming Boxing Day and New Year's Junkanoo parades were already in place.

To the delight of many locals, temperatures had fallen slightly just in time for the celebratory season, but it was still warm enough for visitors to the Bahamas to sunbathe on the powder white beaches and wallow in the clear turquoise sea.

An hour later the elderly couple sat in an attorney's office, a new gold necklace with conch pearl pendant around the woman's neck. "What's all this nonsense about me being incompetent, Arthur?" she asked the attorney. "Gordon and I don't want to be in Nassau any longer than we need to."

"Violet," the attorney leaned towards her on the ornate desk, his shaved mahogany head gleaming as if polished by a shoe shine boy. "As I said when I called you in Scotland, your condo sale was ready to close, but your son came back from Australia and was threatening to mess it up."

The attorney's Bahamian accent still had a trace of British dialect, from the years he had studied law in England. "That's why I asked you to fly out. Jeremy is trying to prove you incompetent, so he can take charge of your estate." He sighed. "He's even talked your daughter into going along with him."

Violet whipped off her hat. Arthur still marvelled at her eyes, as blue as they had been all those years ago when he became her attorney and friend. "Sandra agreed? How could she? I know we've had our differences, but I never expected....."

"Don't worry, lassie," Violet's male companion stroked her arm. He had placed his own hat politely on his lap. "We'll get it all sorted out."

"That we will, Gordon." Violet smiled fondly at him, calming down. "When Harry sent Jeremy off to Australia, I should have known one day he would return with his foul ways – God forgive me for saying that about my own son."

"Your late husband did what was best," the attorney intervened. "You know Jeremy made a fool of himself around town, with all his carousing and drinking."

"Well, I have a new husband now and a new life in Scotland," Violet stated. "And I don't want our remaining time on this earth to be disrupted by a son and daughter who think more of themselves than they do of me."

"I feel the same way about my son," Gordon interjected, fingering the brim of his hat. "None of them wanted us to be together, let alone get married."

"Unfortunately," said the attorney, "Violet's family think you married her for her money."

"I don't need Violet's money," Gordon said indignantly. "I am quite well provided for." He couldn't help it if Violet liked to foot most of the bills. They loved each other and the question of finances never came into their relationship.

"Can they do this?" Violet asked her attorney.

"They can try, but I'm pulling out all the legal stops to prevent them from doing so." The attorney smiled reassuringly at Violet. "Leave it with me and I'll see what I can come up with."

Violet and Gordon strolled back to their hotel. They had decided to treat themselves to a stay in the British Colonial Hilton in downtown Nassau. It had been a toss up between a harbour view where they could look out on the cruise ships anchored nearby or a city view, where they could watch the vibrant Junkanoo street parade that would take place in the early hours of Boxing Day. They planned on being back in Scotland for Hogmanay.

Visitors came from around the world to watch and listen to the sights and sounds of Junkanoo, with its vivid costumes and floats, cowbells, goatskin drums, whistles and horns.

Violet and Gordon opted for a harbour view from the hotel. It reminded them of their escape from Nassau a year ago, when they stayed in a Florida oceanfront hotel en route to Scotland - their first time together without their children's criticism and attempts to break up their relationship.

That night in the British Colonial hotel, as the couple gazed from their room at the moonlight on the shimmering indigo blue sea, Gordon said proudly, as he had never tired of repeating during the past year, 'We tricked them, lassie.'

"We did that," Violet smiled. "They never imagined we'd move to Scotland."

"Not until they found out you'd put your condo up for sale," Gordon laughed.

"Do you think they believed something bad happened to us?"

"I do, lassie!" They both chuckled and snuggled up to each other.

Later, they walked hand in hand down the wide staircase to the Aqua restaurant, where they avoided a lavish buffet and ate a light dinner before retiring to their room for the night.

Bay Street was buzzing the next morning. It was just like a perfect British summer's day, the kind of weather that brought the "snow birds" as they were called, down from Canada and North America, as well as from other parts of the world, to spend the winter months in second homes.

Violet and Gordon explored the little alleyways that connected the main downtown thoroughfare with Woodes Rogers Walk and pushed their way through the Straw Market that bulged with goods. They chose Athena's Restaurant for lunch and ordered Greek gyros.

They didn't bump into anyone they had known from all the years they had lived in Nassau, Violet from birth and Gordon from his early banking days. If they had, one of those friends might have asked, "Playing tourist today?" Many Nassau residents shopped in the newer shopping malls of New Providence rather than in old downtown Nassau, where tourists flocked.

"Time for tea," Violet told Gordon and they headed back to the hotel. They shared a leisurely brew on the pool deck, with a bright blue umbrella shading them from the dazzling sunshine. Violet wistfully watched youngsters her grandchildren's age work off steam in the water.

When they went up to their room for a rest, she told Gordon, "If only they weren't so spoiled."

"Who?" he asked.

"My grandchildren." She pulled back the downy bedspread.

"Och well, you contributed to that," Gordon said.

"You think so?"

"I know so," he said, stretching out on the vast king-sized bed, the piping air conditioning evoking a lazy yawn.

As they were dozing off, the phone rang. Violet picked up the receiver. It was the front desk. "Some people are here to see you, ma'am." To Violet's surprise, the name given her by the clerk was her daughter's.

"Well, I suppose we have to see what she wants," said Violet. They brushed off their clothes and went downstairs to the elegant lobby.

Standing at the bottom of the staircase were Sandra, her two children and Gordon's son. Sandra looked sheepish, but the children ran towards Violet and hugged her around her waist.

"Granny, Granny!" they shouted, with the excitement that only children can portray.

"They've missed you, Mum," Sandra said. She hesitated for a moment. "And we have too."

Several days later when remnants of the Boxing Day Junkanoo were strewn across the downtown streets, Violet and Gordon's plane landed at Heathrow. Sandra had talked her brother into dropping his incompetency suit and Violet's condo sale had closed.

The couple headed for their Glasgow flight connection, wrapped warmly against the winter chill. During the years Gordon flew back to the U.K. on holiday with his young son and first wife, it was always an eye opening moment on entering the terminal when he breathed in the cold air, mingled with the smell of jet fuel. After the easygoing island life that he led in the Bahamas, it pulled him up short, reminding him that he was re-entering a "First World" country with rules and regulations.

As the Glasgow flight took off, they gazed down at the patchwork of snow-crusted fields below. Sandra would be bringing the children to visit them in the spring and Gordon's son might introduce his new lady friend to them during the summer. Jeremy had returned to Australia, but not before he had reconciled with his mother and given her and Gordon his blessing. His change of heart showed he must have learned something from the decades spent in exile down under.

"It was all worth it, don't you think, lassie," the elderly man asked the elderly woman beside him.

"Yes, dear, it was," the elderly woman replied.

* * First published in the December 13th 2013
special "Annual Edition" of *The Lady* magazine,
London, England, as "Twilight Paradise" -
www.lady.co.uk

READ MORE OF VIOLET AND GORDON'S
ESCAPADES IN THE FULL-LENGTH ROMANTIC
SUSPENSE NOVEL "LOVE AT SUNSET" AVAILABLE
AS AN EBOOK AND IN PAPERBACK AT AMAZON
AND OTHER ONLINE RETAILERS!